Snow Angel

To Margaret, Beatrice,
Eugenia, Marion,
and their angels
—J.M.

To my sister Lucy, who was
forgotten at the grocery store.
With special thanks to my models,
Martha and Emma Sawyer and Linda Wemple
—J.R.

Text copyright © 1995 by Jean Marzollo.
Illustrations copyright © 1995 by Jacqueline Rogers.
All rights reserved. Published by Scholastic Inc.
SCHOLASTIC HARDCOVER is a registered trademark of Scholastic Inc.

Library of Congress Cataloging-in-Publication Data
Marzollo, Jean.
    Snow Angel / by Jean Marzollo ; illustrated by Jacqueline Rogers.
        p.   cm.
    Summary: Accidentally left behind in a snowstorm, a young girl is befriended by a snow angel
who takes the girl on a magical flight in search of her mother.
    ISBN 0-590-48748-5
    [1. Snow—Fiction. 2. Angels—Fiction.] I. Rogers, Jacqueline, ill. II. Title.
PZ7.M3688Sn 1995
[E]—dc20
94-31997
                                                                                                                CIP
                                                                                                                AC

12 11 10 9 8 7 6 5 4 3 2 1   5 6 7 8 9/9 0/0
                                        Printed in Singapore   10
                                    First printing, October 1995

Jacqueline Rogers used gouache, watercolors, acrylic colors, and torn paper
to prepare the art for this book.

Snow Angel

BY JEAN MARZOLLO

ILLUSTRATED BY JACQUELINE ROGERS

SCHOLASTIC
HARDCOVER

SCHOLASTIC INC.
New York

There was so much snow
that school closed early.

On with our snowsuits—puff, puff,
On with our boots—pull, pull,
On with our hats—tug, tug.

Outside we waved good-bye to our teacher
standing in a whirl of white.
Good-bye! Good-bye!

There was so much snow
I couldn't see the corner
where my mother was waiting.

But then I saw her old blue station wagon.
And then I saw my sister get in,
and then I saw my brother get in,
and then I saw the kids next door get in, too.

"Wait!" I yelled.
But it was hard to run.
I had to watch where I was going.

Run, run, through the snow.
Whoops!

I slipped and fell down.

When I looked up,
I saw the blue doors shut
and my mother drive away.
She'll turn around
and come back for me,
I thought.
So I waited.

Mama, Mama, don't you know
That you left me in the snow?

The crossing guard
was new and loud.
"Stop right there!" he said.

I stepped back
and back again
into someone's yard
where I waited.
After a while, I lay down.
Feathers of snow
tickled my cheeks
and made me blink.

I moved my arms and legs
to make a snow angel.

Mama, Mama, don't you know?
I'm an angel in the snow.

I stood up carefully
so I wouldn't mess my angel,
but when I looked down,
she wasn't there.
She was standing up, too,
and she looked like me.

Only instead of wearing
a snowsuit, mittens, and boots,
she was wearing
a long silver dress
and Jack Frost wings.

"Let's find your mother," she said,
reaching for my hand.
Through my mitten
I could feel a wonderful warmth.

We lifted off the ground
and flew over houses,
stores, and trees.

Mama, Mama, don't you know?
I am flying through the snow.

I squinted to see the cars below—
red ones, black ones,
green ones, a blue one.
"There it is!" I shouted.

My angel and I swooped down
until we were flying right over our car.
We followed the car into the driveway
and landed on the roof.
All the doors opened.

"Mama!" I shouted. "Mama!"
"She can't hear you," said my angel,
"but you can hear her."

"Where's Jamie?" said my mother.
"Oh, dear! I left her at school!
Children, go in and take off your snowsuits.
Tell Grandpa I went back to get Jamie!"

"Mama!" I cried. "I'm up here!"

My mother looked up and said,
"I've never seen so much snow!"

"She can't see you when you're with me,"
said my angel, "but she will see you soon."

Mama, Mama, don't you know?
I'm above you in the snow.

We flew ahead and landed
on the spot where I had met my angel.

The blue station wagon was coming
down the street.
I jumped up and waved.
Then I asked my new friend,
"Can you come home with me?"
"My home is in the snow," she said.
"And now I must return."
My angel waved good-bye
and disappeared.

Quick as can be, I lay down
and moved my arms and legs.
"Come back!" I cried.
But when I stood up,
all I saw was a mess of snow
on the ground.

Honk! Honk!
The car pulled up.
My mother jumped out and hugged me.
"You poor thing!
Waiting all this time in a blizzard!
I feel terrible!
Did you think I forgot all about you?"

"Not really," I said.

In the car my mother asked more questions.
"Are you sure you're all right?
What did you do all that time
you were waiting?"

"I made up a poem," I said
in a soft, snowy voice.

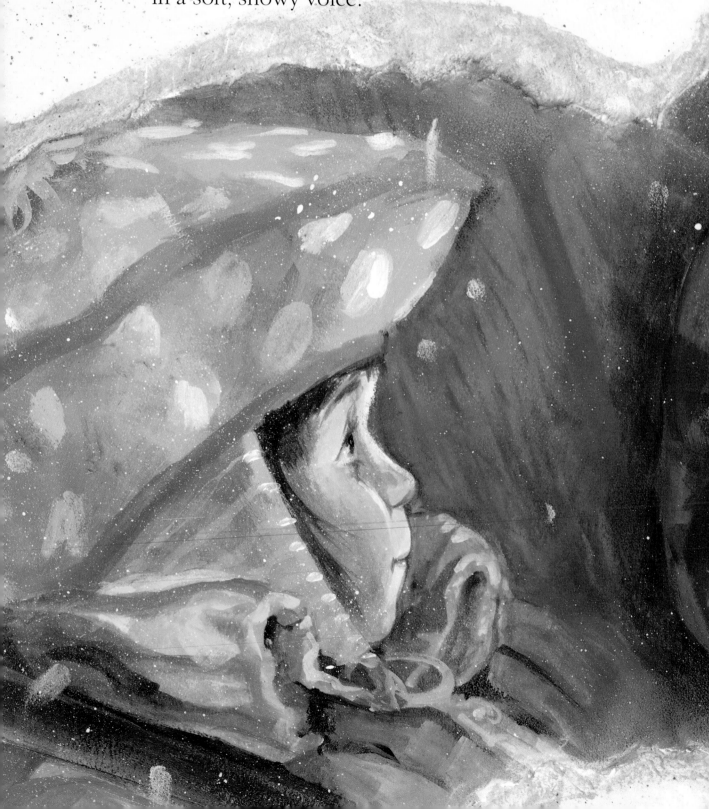

Mama, Mama, don't you know?
I could see you in the snow.
Mama, Mama, don't you know?
I could hear you in the snow.
Mama, Mama, don't you know?
I was with you in the snow.
Mama, Mama, don't you know?
There are angels made of snow.